PUFFIN BOOKS

Published by the Penguin Group
Penguin Books Ltd, 80 Strand, London WC2R 0RL, England
Penguin Group (USA) Inc., 375 Hudson Street, New York, New York 10014, USA
Penguin Group (Canada), 90 Eglinton Avenue East, Suite 700, Toronto, Ontario, Canada M4P 2Y3 (a division of Pearson Penguin Canada Inc.)
Penguin Ireland, 25 St Stephen's Green, Dublin 2, Ireland (a division of Penguin Books Ltd)
Penguin Group (Australia) Ltd, 707 Collins Street, Melbourne, Victoria 3008, Australia
Penguin Books India Pvt Ltd, 11 Community Centre, Panchsheel Park, New Delhi – 110 017, India
Penguin Group (NZ), 67 Apollo Drive, Rosedale, North Shore 0632, New Zealand (a division of Pearson New Zealand Ltd)
Penguin Books (South Africa) (Pty) Ltd, Block D, Rosebank Office Park, 181 Jan Smuts Avenue, Parktown North, Gauteng 2193, South Africa

Penguin Books Ltd, Registered Offices: 80 Strand, London WC2R 0RL, England

puffinbooks.com

First published in the USA by Henry Holt and Company, Inc, 1991
Published in Great Britain by Hamish Hamilton Ltd 1992
Published in Puffin Books 1994
Published in this edition 2011
008

Text copyright © Bill Martin Jr, 1991. Text copyright © the Estate of Bill Martin Jr, 2004
Illustrations copyright © Eric Carle, 1991
All rights reserved

The moral right of the author and illustrator has been asserted

Made and printed in China

British Library Cataloguing in Publication Data
A CIP catalogue record for this book is available from the British Library
ISBN: 978–0–141–33481–3

For more information about Eric Carle or his books, please visit eric-carle.com
The Eric Carle Museum of Picture Book Art was built to celebrate the art that we are first exposed to as children. Located in Amherst,
Massachusetts, in the United States of America, the 40,000-square-foot museum is devoted to national and international picture book art.
Visit carlemuseum.org

Polar Bear, Polar Bear, What Do You Hear?

By Bill Martin Jr
Pictures by Eric Carle

PUFFIN

Polar Bear, Polar Bear,
what do you hear?

I hear a lion
roaring in my ear.

Lion, Lion,
what do you hear?

I hear a hippopotamus
snorting in my ear.

Hippopotamus, Hippopotamus,
what do you hear?

I hear a flamingo
fluting in my ear.

Flamingo, Flamingo,
what do you hear?

I hear a zebra
braying in my ear.

Zebra, Zebra,
what do you hear?

I hear a boa constrictor
hissing in my ear.

Boa Constrictor, Boa Constrictor,
what do you hear?

I hear an elephant
trumpeting in my ear.

Elephant, Elephant,
what do you hear?

I hear a leopard
snarling in my ear.

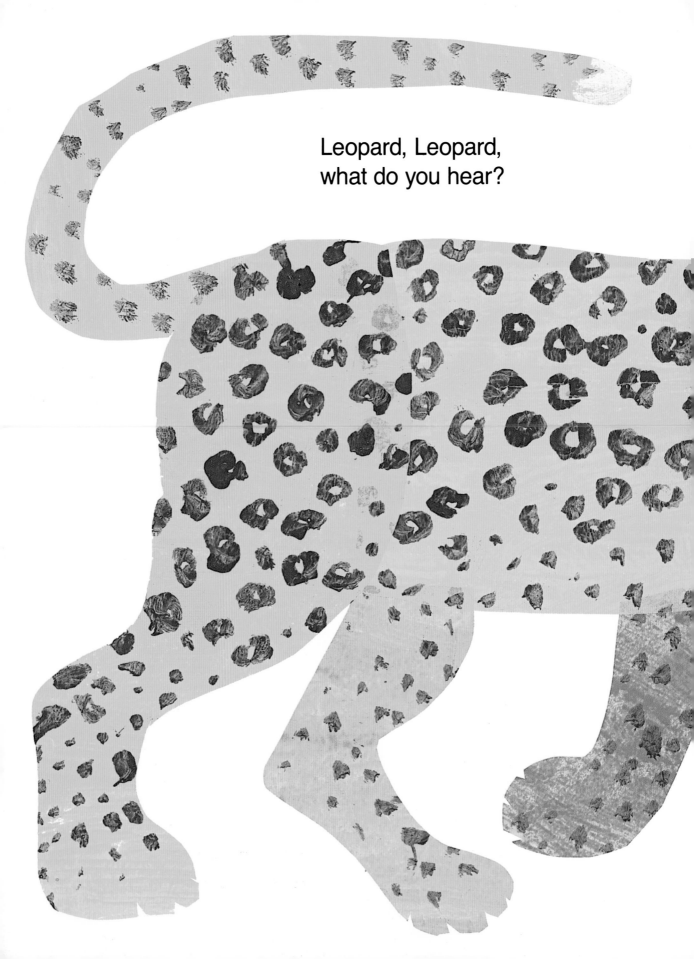

Leopard, Leopard,
what do you hear?

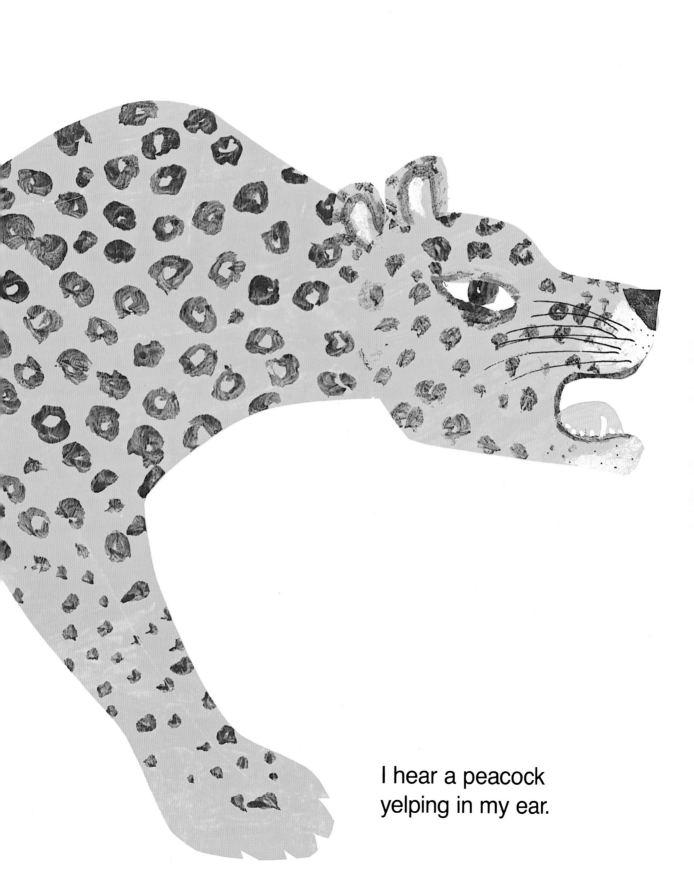

I hear a peacock
yelping in my ear.

Peacock, Peacock,
what do you hear?

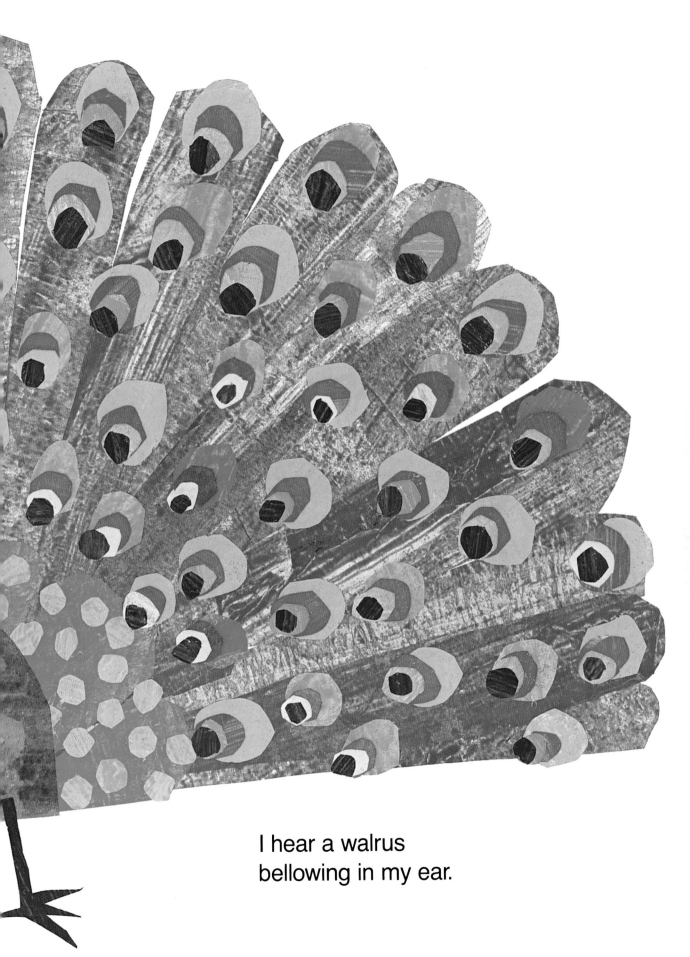

I hear a walrus
bellowing in my ear.

Walrus, Walrus,
what do you hear?

I hear a zookeeper
whistling in my ear.

Zookeeper, Zookeeper,
what do you hear?

I hear children . . .

. . . growling like a polar bear,
roaring like a lion,
snorting like a hippopotamus,
fluting like a flamingo,
braying like a zebra,
hissing like a boa constrictor,
trumpeting like an elephant,
snarling like a leopard,
yelping like a peacock,
bellowing like a walrus . . .

that's what I hear.

Other titles in the series

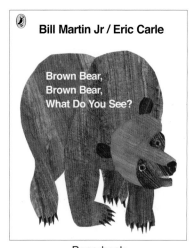

Bill Martin Jr / Eric Carle

Brown Bear,
Brown Bear,
What Do You See?

Paperback
ISBN: 978–0–141–50159–8

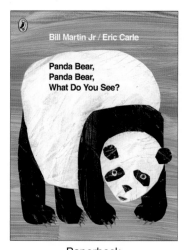

Bill Martin Jr / Eric Carle

Panda Bear,
Panda Bear,
What Do You See?

Paperback
ISBN: 978–0–141–50145–1

Bill Martin Jr / Eric Carle

Baby Bear,
Baby Bear,
What Do You See?

Paperback
ISBN: 978–0–141–38445–0

Also by Eric Carle

THE VERY HUNGRY CATERPILLAR
by Eric Carle

Paperback
ISBN: 978–0–140–56932–2

COUNT
with
The Very Hungry Caterpillar

includes GIANT reusable STICKERS!

Sticker book
ISBN: 978–0–141–50196–3

little learning library

Board book slipcase
ISBN: 978–0–141–38511–2

Eric Carle   THE VERY HUNGRY CATERPILLAR
POP-UP BOOK

Novelty hardback
ISBN: 978–0–141–38506–8

The Bad-Tempered Ladybird
Eric Carle

Paperback
ISBN: 978–0–141–33203–1

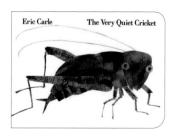

Eric Carle   The Very Quiet Cricket

Board book
ISBN: 978–0–241–13785–7

Eric Carle   The Very Busy Spider

Board book
ISBN: 978–0–241–13590–7